Noisy Poems for a Busy Day

Written by Robert Heidbreder

Illustrated by Lori Joy Smith

Kids Can Press

Contents

Out of Bed

Riffle-rustle,
feet down-pound.
Another day
has rolled around!

Yeah!

5

Off to Breakfast

Scrunchy munch-up.
Sloppy slurp.
Swibble down.
Big belch — BURP!

"What do you say?"

"Excuse me!"

BURP!

Teeth Need Brushing

Bristle-thistle.
Toothy rub.
Chompers get
a sun-up scrub.

Smile!

7

On with Clothes

Twisty-twiggle.
Jump-up jiggle.
Undies backward!
Wiggle-giggle.

Hee! Hee!

Out to Play

Bangity-slam.
Leap-spring wide.
Kiss the morning
air outside.

Kiss-kiss!

Doggie Hi

Slip-slap-lick.
Big wet SMOOCH!
Doggie loves me.
I love pooch.

   Hug-hug!

Somersaults

Tipsy-topsy.
Turvy-curve.
Swirly-curly.
Tumble-swerve.

Cool!

11

Cloud Watch

Puffy stuffies,
dragon drifters,
duelling dogs —
sky shape-shifters.

Bumble-tumble ...

13

Treetop Climb

Shimmy-jimmy,
clutchy-creep.
Climb up tree,
scary-steep!

Whoa, down there!

14

Listen, Listen

Crissle-sissle.
Twitter-tweet.
Wind and bird
thrum a soft beat.

Thip! Thip! Shhh!

15

Now Back Down

Bummy-wiggle.
Slip-down ... THUD!
Gurpy-slurpy.
Hello, mud!

Plop!

16

DIRTY!

Squishy-squash.
Muddy flop.
Hop to house.
Pull door and —

"STOP!"

"Why?"

17

Out of Clothes

Jump-up jiggle.
Sniggle-giggle.
Clean clothes on.
Twisty-twiggle.

Hee!

Ha!

Ho!

Time for Lunch

Scrunchy munch-up.
Sloppy slurp.
Swibble down.
Big belch — BURP!

"What do you say?"

"Excuse me!"

"And?"

"Thank you!"

19

Off to Park

A scoot-skip round.
A rush headlong.
Sing a noisy
park-bound song:

La-la-la-la-lee-lee!

Pick a Stick

Ala-ka-zee!
Ala-ka-zopper!
See me be
a big grasshopper!

Zip!

Hip! Hop!

To Sky-Swings

Swish-swash-swirr.
Higher, HIGHER!
Swing-wing up
to sun's hot fire!

Whish-whish! Wow!

22

Slide Down

One big launch —
Ziff-zim-zoom!
One second gone!
Crash landing —

BOOM!

Ouch!

24

Then Play Tag

"Get me!" "Gotcha!"
"Hey, no fair."
"I gotcha sure!
All fair and square!"

"NOOOOO!"

25

MAD!

Push-shove-budge.
Tongues stuck out!
Kids are spatting.
Grown-ups shout:

"OK, children. That's enough! Stop it now."

All Over

"Sorry!"
"Sorry!"
Shake hands, friend.
Shoving, shouting's
at an end.

"OK?"

"OK!"

27

Head Back Home

Shilly-shimmy.
Bop along.
Hum a happy
homeward song:

Hmm-a hmm-a hee ...

29

Dinner Time

Scrunchy munch-up.
Sloppy slurp.
Swibble down.
Big belch — BURP!

    "What do you say?"

        "Excuse me!"

"And?"

        "Thank you!"

"And?"

        "It was good?"

"And?"

        "Can I help clean up?"

"*May* I?"

        "OK!"

Pat the Kitty

Pat the cat —
mauw-mew-purr.
Snuggle-huggle
in its fur.

Soft!

Into Tub

Flish-a-flush.
Splish-splosh rub.
Scrub-a-dub
in bubbly tub.

Splash-splash!

33

Into PJs

Giggle-wiggle.
Jump-in jiggle.
PJs backward —
twisty-twiggle.

Shimmy-shake!

And Teeth Brushing

Whistle-bristle.
Toothpaste line.
Chompers get
a moonbright shine.

'Night!

Into Bed

Slip-in slide.
Pillow pile.
Stuffies near.
Day-done smile.

Ahhhhh!

36

Story Time

Chitter-chatter.
Monkey-tricks.
Fall asleep
in three quick ticks.

Zzzzzzzzzzzzzzz ...

A Dream-filled Head

Flipping, floating
through the air.
Dazzle-dreams
drift everywhere.

Whee!

To Jane, Tikki and Carmela, with happy, busy, noisy affection — R.H.

To Paul, Sosi and Ila, for making my days noisy, busy and so full of love — L. J. S.

Text © 2012 Robert Heidbreder
Illustrations © 2012 Lori Joy Smith

Kids Can Press acknowledges the financial support of the Government of Ontario, through the Ontario Media Development Corporation's Ontario Book Initiative; the Ontario Arts Council; the Canada Council for the Arts; and the Government of Canada, through the BPIDP, for our publishing activity.

Published in Canada by
Kids Can Press Ltd.
25 Dockside Drive
Toronto, ON M5A 0B5

Published in the U.S. by
Kids Can Press Ltd.
2250 Military Road
Tonawanda, NY 14150

www.kidscanpress.com

The artwork in this book was rendered in pencil and colored in Photoshop.
The text is set in Cronos Pro.

Edited by Yvette Ghione
Designed by Marie Bartholomew

This book is smyth sewn casebound.
Manufactured in China, in 4/2012, through Asia Pacific Offset, 3/F, New factory (No.12), Jing Yi Industrial Center, Tian Bei Estate, Fu Ming Community, Guan Lan, Bao An, Shenzhen, China

CM 12 0 9 8 7 6 5 4 3 2 1

Library and Archives Canada Cataloguing in Publication

Heidbreder, Robert
    Noisy poems for a busy day / written by Robert
Heidbreder ; illustrated by Lori Joy Smith.

ISBN 978-1-55453-706-8

    I. Smith, Lori Joy, 1973– II. Title.

PS8565.E42N65 2012   jC811'.54   C2011-906994-6

Kids Can Press is a **lorus**™ Entertainment company